I HAVE A FRIEND

I HAVE A FRIEND

Keiko Narahashi

MARGARET K. McELDERRY BOOKS

for Micah

The original pictures for *I Have a Friend* are watercolor paintings.

Margaret K. McElderry Books
An imprint of Simon & Schuster Children's Publishing Division
1230 Avenue of the Americas
New York, New York 10020
Copyright © 1967 by Keiko Narahashi
All rights reserved including the right of reproduction
in whole or in part in any form.

Composition by Linoprint Composition, New York, New York
Printed and bound by Toppan Printing in China

First Edition
10 9 8 7 6 5 4 3

Library of Congress Cataloging-in-Publication Data

Narahashi, Keiko.
I have a friend.

Summary: A small boy tells about his friend who
lives with him, who follows him, who sometimes is
very tall, but who disappears when the sun goes down—
his shadow.

[1. Shadows—Fiction] I. Title.
PZ7.N158Iab 1987   [E]   86-27628
ISBN 0-689-50432-2

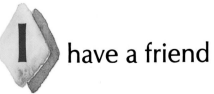 have a friend

who lives

in my house.

He sits with me on the steps

and follows me down the street…

to the park, where he hides in the trees

and whispers in my ear, "You can't catch me!"

In the summertime we are at the beach.

He swims underwater, dancing and shaking
and never holding still...

even when

I hold my breath.

Sometimes he is short and fat.

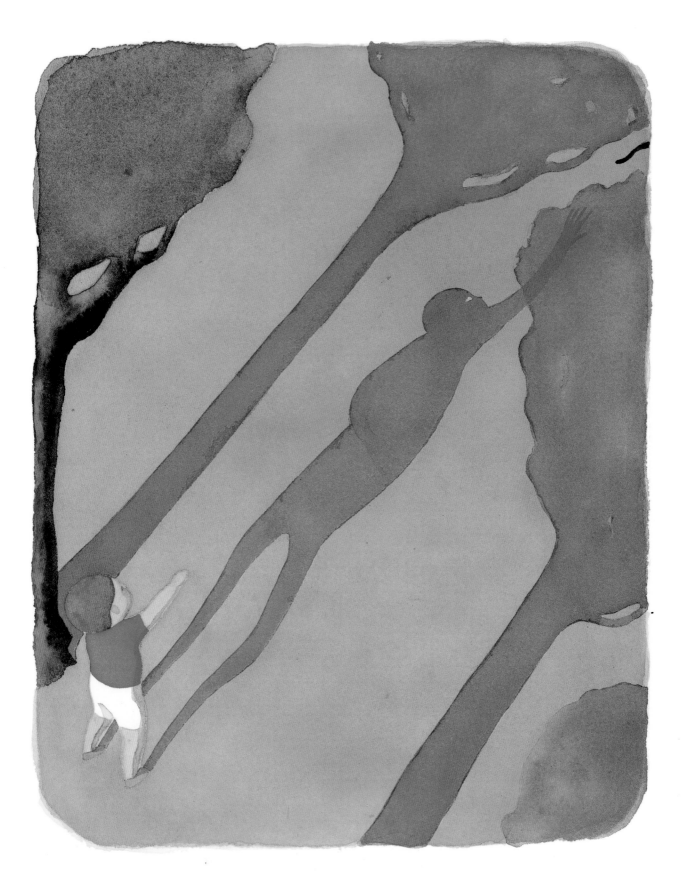

And sometimes he is so tall he can touch the treetops.

He can slide up a wall

or hip-hop down the stairs.

He warns the butterflies

when I am near.

He goes places I can't follow.

He keeps my dreams secret and safe.

But when the sun goes down,

he disappears into the darkness.

Night falls...

and I go home.

In the morning

he will be waiting with the sun.

He is yesterday's night

left behind for the day.